TITANIC

ARTHUR McKEOWN

ILLUSTRATED BY PETER HOGAN

READY-TO-READ

ALADDIN PAPERBACKS

First Aladdin Paperbacks Edition July 1998

Text copyright © 1996 by Arthur McKeown
Illustrations copyright © 1996 by Peter Hogan

Originally published in Ireland by Poolbeg Press Ltd, Dublin

Aladdin Paperbacks
An imprint of Simon & Schuster
Children's Publishing Division
1230 Avenue of the Americas
New York, NY 10020

Printed and bound in the United States of America
10 9 8 7 6 5 4 3 2 1

Library of Congress Cataloging-in-Publication Data
McKeown, Arthur.
Titanic / Arthur McKeown ; illustrated by Peter Hogan.—1st Aladdin Paperbacks ed.
p.   cm.—(Ready-to-read)
"Originally published in Ireland by Poolbeg Press Ltd., Dublin."
Summary: In 1912, Mary is on board the Titanic when it hits
an iceberg and changes her life forever.
ISBN 0-689-82476-9
1. Titanic (Steamship)—Juvenile fiction.   [1. Titanic (Steamship)—Fiction.
2. Shipwrecks—Fiction.   3. Ocean liners—Fiction.]
I. Hogan, Peter, ill.   II. Title.   III. Series.
PZ7. M4786765Ti   1998
[Fic]—dc21   98-7951
CIP   AC

For Jane and Andrew, again
AM

For MC and NJ
PH

CONTENTS

1	The *Titanic* Leaves Belfast	6
2	Mary on the *Titanic*	12
3	The *Titanic* at Sea	19
4	The *Titanic* Hits an Iceberg	26
5	Mary in America	38

THE TITANIC LEAVES BELFAST

"Hurrah! Hurrah!"

Everyone was cheering and clapping. Men threw their caps high in the air. "Good luck! Good luck!" they shouted.

It was just after twelve o'clock on a sunny
morning nearly one hundred years ago. The
Titanic moved slowly down into the water of
Belfast Lough. She was a huge ship. She was
very fast and very strong.

"This ship can't sink," said Mr. Andrews. He built her for Harland and Wolff in Belfast. "She's the best ship in the world. A Belfast ship is the biggest and the strongest and the best ship in the whole world!"

The *Titanic* had all the latest inventions. She had a radio to talk to other ships. There was a big swimming pool for the passengers and Turkish baths and a library and a barber's shop. In the gym there was an electric horse to help passengers who wanted to get fit. There was even a special kennel for the Captain's dog!

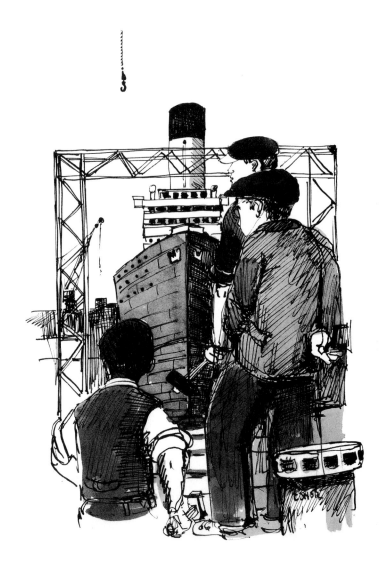

It took more than nine months to finish the great ship after her launch. One morning, at the beginning of April 1912, all the work was completed. At last she was ready for sea.

The *Titanic*'s great engines roared as the huge
ship set out for Southampton.

MARY ON THE TITANIC

At Southampton lots of passengers got on board. There was a lot of noise. Everyone was busy and very excited.

Mary was with her mother and father. She was very excited, too. She was going to visit her aunt and uncle in New York. She was looking forward to seeing all her cousins.

"Hurry up, Mary!" said her mother. "We must go on board and see our cabins."

Their cabins were comfortable. There was a
big room for her parents and a small room for
her.

"Come on, Mary!" said her father. "Let's go
and watch the Captain get ready for sea."

Captain Smith was in charge of the *Titanic*. He
was tall and had a big white beard. He had
been a sailor for over 40 years. This was his
last trip before he retired.

Captain Smith was on the bridge of the *Titanic* with Mr. Andrews. They were watching as the crew made everything ready for sea.

"Hello, Mary," said Captain Smith. "This is the biggest ship in the whole world! We must get ready for our passengers. There are lots of rich and famous people. Some are bankers and businessmen; some are teachers and lawyers; others work on the railways. Our passengers must have the best – the best food and the best music and everything! This ship is better than the best hotel in Europe or America."

Mary watched as men carried the boxes on board. There were 35 tons of fresh meat and 40 tons of potatoes and 12,000 dinner plates and 35,000 fresh eggs and 45,000 napkins – lots and lots of everything!

THE TITANIC AT SEA

The *Titanic* left Southampton at noon. The sky was bright and clear. Hundreds of people stood and watched the ship move slowly out to sea. They cheered and clapped.

The great ship moved into the deep water. Then she set off for France. More passengers came aboard there. She called at Cork, then left Ireland for the last time.

The *Titanic*'s great engines roared as she set out to cross the deep, cold waters of the Atlantic to America.

During the journey the passengers had a wonderful time. In the morning they sat in deck chairs in the sunshine or went for a walk around the ship talking to each other. Others used the swimming pool or the Turkish bath. Some even tried out the new electric horse for exercise to get fit.

In the afternoon the passengers had tea in the Café Parisien or in their cabins.

After dinner in the evening there was music and dancing in the ballroom. The band played all sorts of bright, cheerful music. The ladies wore beautiful dresses. Everyone was happy and having a wonderful time.

Mary sat in a corner and watched everything.
She thought it was wonderful. She felt like a
princess.

Then it was time for Mary to go to bed. She was tired but very happy.

In her cabin she said her prayers with her father.

"Good night, Mary," said her mother and father. "Sleep tight. God bless!"

THE TITANIC HITS AN ICEBERG

After five days the *Titanic* was hundreds of miles from land. It was the evening of Sunday, April 14th.

The weather got colder. The Captain of another ship saw a lot of big icebergs where he was. He sent a radio message about them to Captain Smith.

The stars were out. There was no moon. It was
a fine, clear night. There was very little wind.
The sea was as smooth as glass.

The *Titanic* hit an iceberg just before midnight. The ship shook when she collided with the huge mountain of ice.

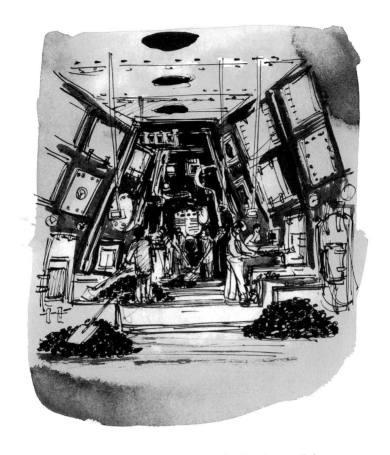

Some people came out of their cabins to see what was going on. A few passengers screamed, but no one panicked. The ship's lights flickered but did not go out. The crew worked hard and kept them going so everyone could see.

"Don't worry!" shouted Captain Smith.

People rushed about. Some boys and girls were crying. They held on tightly to their mothers and fathers.

"Stop running around!" Captain Smith ordered. "Get into the lifeboats! Women and children first!"

Mary held on tightly to her mother's hand. They went along the deck. It was cold. Mary was frightened. They reached a lifeboat.

"Come along, Mary!" said her mother. "We have to get off the ship."

"But what about Daddy?" asked Mary. "We can't leave him."

"He can't come," said her mother sadly. "He's staying with Captain Smith and Mr. Andrews and the other men."

Mary and her mother got into one of the
lifeboats.

The ship's band came out on deck. They started to play. At first they played bright, cheerful music. After a while they started to play hymns instead.

The lifeboat with Mary and her mother moved away from the *Titanic*. They watched as the huge ship sank slowly into the dark water.

After three hours the cold water covered the
ship. The *Titanic* had sunk deep into the cold,
black water of the Atlantic.

Other ships raced to help the passengers who
were in the lifeboats. They took them to New York.

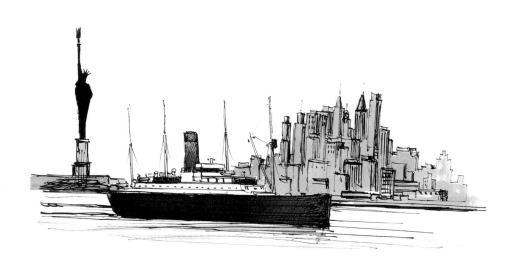

MARY IN AMERICA

Mary and her mother arrived in New York three days later. They were tired and very sad. Mary's aunt and uncle were so glad to see them!

Mary's picture was in every newspaper.

A lot of people died when the *Titanic* sank. There had not been enough lifeboats to save all the passengers and crew who were on the ship. Some of the passengers and crew were able to get away. They got into the lifeboats. They were saved by other ships that came to help them.

Mary never saw her father again. He was one of the passengers who drowned when the *Titanic* sank.

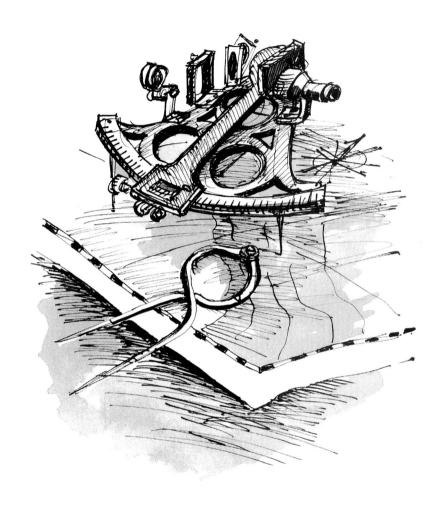

Captain Smith went down with his ship. He was last seen helping to put a small child into one of the lifeboats.

Mr. Andrews also drowned when the *Titanic* sank. He had tried to help everyone – except himself.

He was last seen throwing deck chairs over the
side of the ship, so that people would have
something to help them float in the water.

There were eight workmen from Harland and Wolff on the *Titanic*. Seven drowned. But one man, Alfred Cunningham, was rescued from the water and taken to New York.

2,201 people were on board the *Titanic*. 1,489 people drowned when the great ship sank. 712 people were rescued.

Mary stayed in America with her cousins. She grew up and got married. She became a mother and then a grandmother. She had lots of grandchildren.

But she never forgot the terrible night the *Titanic* sank and changed her life forever.